SHARING WITH OTHERS

A Book about Selfishness

CAROLYN LARSEN
ILLUSTRATED BY TIM O'CONNOR

BakerBooks
a division of Baker Publishing Group
Grand Rapids, Michigan

Text © 2017 by Carolyn Larsen
Illustrations © 2017 by Baker Publishing Group

Published by Baker Books
a division of Baker Publishing Group
P.O. Box 6287, Grand Rapids, MI 49516-6287
www.bakerbooks.com

Printed in the United States of America

Library of Congress Cataloging-in-Publication Data
Names: Larsen, Carolyn, 1950– author.
Title: Sharing with others : a book about selfishness / Carolyn
    Larsen ; illustrated by Tim O'Connor.
Description: Grand Rapids : Baker Books, 2017. | Series:
    Growing God's kids
Identifiers: LCCN 2016033230 | ISBN 9780801009600 (pbk.)
Subjects: LCSH: Selfishness—Juvenile literature. | Sharing in
    children—Juvenile literature.
Classification: LCC BJ1535.S4 L37 2017 | DDC 177/.7—dc23
LC record available at https://lccn.loc.gov/2016033230

Scripture quotation is from the *Holy Bible*, New Living Translation, copyright © 1996, 2004, 2015 by Tyndale House Foundation. Used by permission of Tyndale House Publishers, Inc., Carol Stream, Illinois 60188. All rights reserved.

18   19   20   21   22   23   7   6   5   4   3   2

"Don't be selfish;
don't try to impress others.
Be humble, thinking of others
as better than yourselves."

———————————

PHILIPPIANS 2:3

See that boy? That's Max. Most of the time Max is a nice boy, but once in a while he thinks only about himself. That is called selfishness.

My name is Leonard and I'm Max's favorite toy.

want to play with trucks in the sandbox," Max
says.

"And you have to do what I want to do," he tells
his friends.

"We want to play on the playground today," Max's friends say.

"No! I want to play with trucks! You have to stay here!" Max says.

Max doesn't care what his friends want to do.

Max thinks what he wants is more important than what his friends want. That leads to an argument with his friends.

Mom says Max should suggest a compromise. So, Max asks his friends if they want to play with trucks after playing on the playground first.

Don't be selfish.
Philippians 2:3

Grandma sent a present to Max and his brother. It's a cool airplane. Grandma said they should share it.

But Max won't share. He wants the airplane all to himself.

Max is being selfish. He won't share with Zach.

He thinks he should get to play with the airplane as long as he wants. He doesn't care that Grandma said to share the toy.

"Grandma sent the airplane to both of you," Mom says. "You must give Zach a chance to play with it, too. I know it's hard to share because you like it so much. But you would be upset if Zach didn't share it with you, right?"

She was right. Max gave the airplane to Zach.

Don't be selfish.
Philippians 2:3

Max has lots and lots of toys. He has so many that he can't play with them all. He hasn't played with some of them in a long time.

Mom asks, "Would you like to give some toys to children who don't have any toys?"

Max says, "No."

Max wants to keep all of his toys for himself.
Even the ones he doesn't like anymore.

Max is being very selfish.

Mom says, "Think what it would be like to not have any toys. Some families can't afford to buy toys."

Max thinks about those children. He feels sad for them.

Max decides sharing his toys is the right thing to do.

Don't be selfish.
Philippians 2:3

Dad says that everyone in the family should help with chores.

He assigns chores to each member of the family.
Max's chore is to pick up sticks in the yard before
Dad cuts the grass.

Max wants to play instead of helping the family.

He sits on the step and pouts instead of helping.

Max is being selfish and disobedient.

Dad is working. Mom is working. Zach is working. Sarah is working.

Max doesn't want to be selfish, so he helps his family even though he would rather be playing.

Don't be selfish.
Philippians 2:3

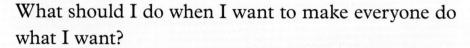

What should I do when I want to make everyone do what I want?

1. Remember that it is kind to think about what others want to do.
2. Think about how it makes me feel mad when someone tries to make me do what they want.
3. Understand that I am being selfish and hurting others' feelings when I insist on having my own way.

How can I be unselfish with my things?

1. Think about how it makes others feel sad when I don't share.
2. Think of games to play with others as I share my toys.
3. Make a chart that shows I get the toy for 15 minutes, then someone else has it for 15 minutes so everyone gets a turn.

What should I do when I want to keep all my things for myself?

1. Think about how I would feel if I lost all my toys.

2. Remember that every child enjoys toys.

3. Understand that giving my toys away is a way to show God's love to others.

What can I do when I don't want to help my family?

1. Think about how hard my parents work to take care of me.

2. Make up games or contests to make doing chores more fun.

3. Remember that helping the family is a way of showing them that I love them.

Remember

God says that real love is not selfish.

God says that loving people pleases him.

God knows that it's not easy to be unselfish, but I can ask for his help.

Sometimes it is not easy to be unselfish. Helping and sharing is a good way of showing God's love to others.

Don't be selfish.
Philippians 2:3